A Kitten is Born

A Kitten is Born

by Heiderose & Andreas Fischer-Nagel

translated by Andrea Mernan

G. P. Putnam's Sons / New York

First American edition.
First published by Kinderbuchverlag Reich, Lucerne, 1982,
under the title EIN KÄTZCHEN KOMMT ZUR WELT.
Copyright © 1983 by Heiderose and Andreas Fischer-Nagel.
All rights reserved. Published simultaneously in
Canada by General Publishing Co. Limited, Toronto.
Printed in the United States of America
Library of Congress Cataloging in Publication Data
Fischer-Nagel, Heiderose.
A kitten is born.
Translation of: Ein Kätzchen kommt zur Welt.
Summary: Text and pictures follow Tabitha's kittens from their
conception and birth to independence from their mother.
1. Kittens—Juvenile literature. 2. Cats—Parturition
—Juvenile literature. [1. Cats. 2. Birth]
I. Fischer-Nagel, Andreas. II. Title.
SF445.7.F5713   1983   636.8'08926   83-4601
ISBN 0-399-20961-1
Second impression.

A Kitten is Born

Our family has a grey-striped cat named Tabitha and we think she is the most beautiful cat in the world.

Tabitha had her first kittens last year when she was a year old. She had a litter of two, and we gave them to friends when they were old enough to leave their mother.

Now Tabitha is ready to have more kittens and this time the father will be the handsome half-angora cat that lives next door.

We know that Tabitha is ready for another litter because she starts acting restless, rolling over on her back and meowing loudly to attract attention. This is a sign that she is in heat and ready to mate with the father. This happens twice a year. After Tabitha and the father have mated, she goes back to being her old self, playing or hunting in the garden or sleeping in the sun on the windowsill.

At first, Tabitha looks the same even though the kittens are begin-
ning to grow inside her. They will be born in about eight or nine
weeks. Only about a month before the birth does her belly start to look
rounder and heavier as the kittens get bigger. Tabitha could have as
many as eight kittens, but she will probably have two or three.

When it is time for the birth, Tabitha looks for a safe, quiet place, such as in a closet or under a bed. But we give her some soft cushions to lie on and because she trusts us, she accepts them.

Just before the kittens are born, a light, clear liquid trickles out of the opening to the birth canal under her tail. Inside their mother, the kittens have been contained in a sac of fluid that protects them from any bumps or jolts. Now it has broken, allowing the first kitten to push through the opening. The kitten is wet and tiny and its eyes are tightly closed. Immediately Tabitha licks her kitten until it is clean and dry. Its eyes will stay closed for about ten days.

The tiny kitten is still connected to its mother by the umbilical cord. It was fed through this cord during the eight weeks it was inside its mother. Now Tabitha bites the cord apart.

The kitten crawls up to its mother's belly, where it finds nipples full of warm milk. The kitten will nurse for about eight weeks until it no longer needs its mother's milk and is eating and drinking on its own.

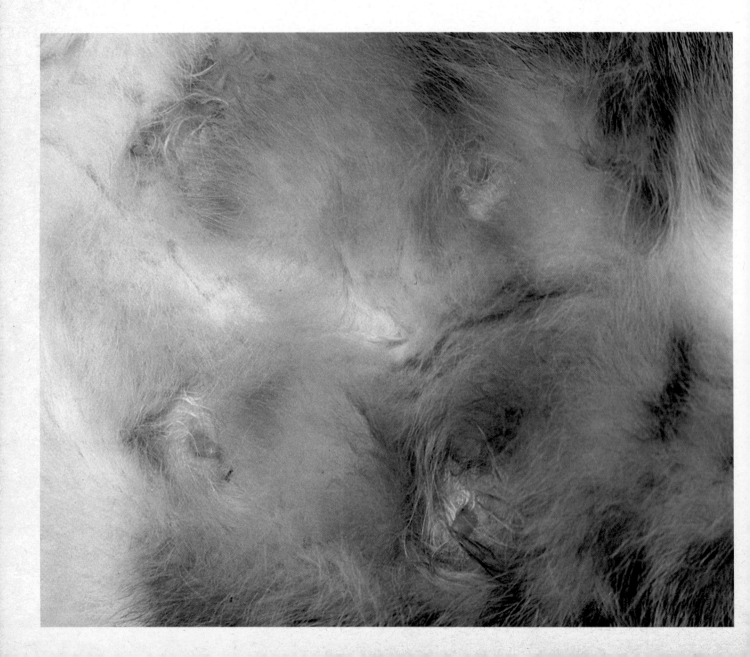

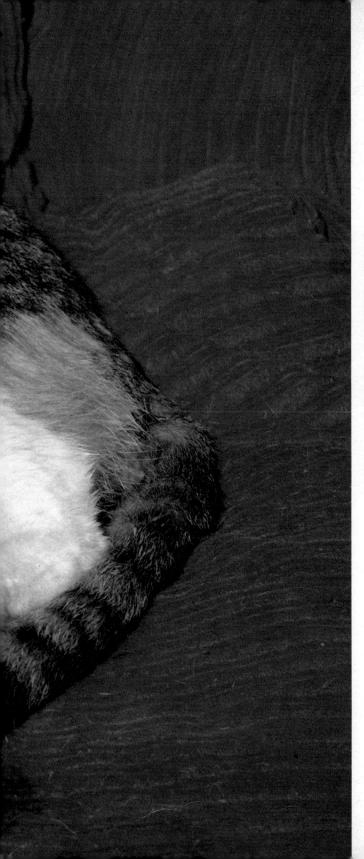

But there are two more kittens still to be born. Tabitha lies down and another kitten comes sliding out of the birth canal, much faster even than the first one.

Tabitha just has time to lick it clean and dry and cut the cord when the third kitten is born.

Tabitha takes care of her last little kitten before she completely cleans and dries herself. Here we can see what is left of the umbilical cord right in the middle of the kitten's pink belly.

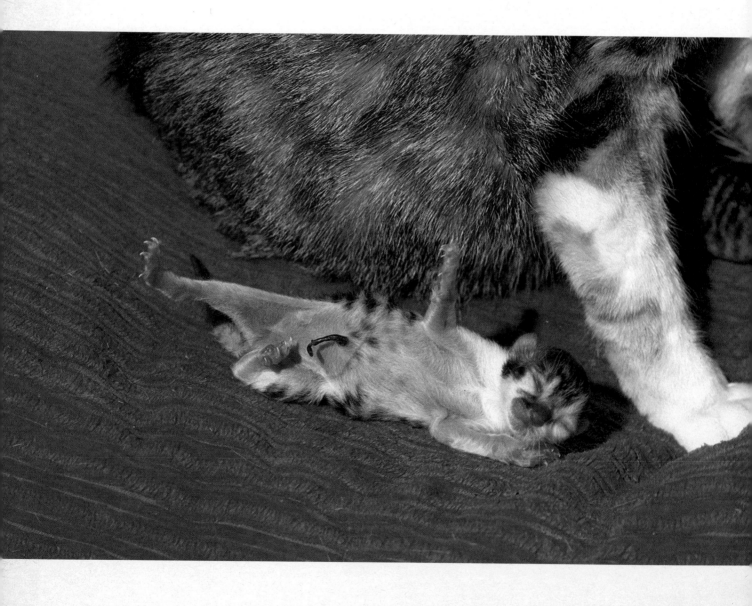

Tabitha curls up contentedly on the pillow to rest and to let her newborn kittens nurse. They lie so close together that it is hard to tell one from another. Each kitten weighs about 3½ oz., about the same as a large chicken egg.

All day we keep going in to look at the kittens. But if we go in too often, or make too much noise, Tabitha will try and move her kittens to a safer place. She grasps them by the skin at the back of their necks and gently carries them away, one at a time. They hang very still in their mother's mouth.

For the first few days, the kittens are a little unsteady as they try to crawl around the cushions. But as their eyes begin to open, they get more sure of themselves and begin to play with each other.

Unlike Tabitha's eyes, which are green, their eyes are all very blue. It will be a few months before they change color.

Tabitha is a good mother. She plays with her kittens and she cleans them from top to bottom. They are still too young to use a litter box.

Now the kittens are bright and alert, with their eyes wide open. They play, sometimes trampling each other with their back paws, sometimes biting one another gently. They tumble about the pillows with their needle-sharp claws catching on the pillows. Kittens can't pull in their claws the way grown cats can.

The kitten on the left is looking into the sun, and its pupils have narrowed to slits, giving it a menacing look. The spunky little kitten on the right tries to scare us away with a hiss when we take a picture.

The kittens are old enough to go out into the garden with Tabitha. This is a strange new world and they blink in the bright sunlight and sniff curiously at the grass and the daisies.

The kittens love to stalk one another. When they are older, they will hunt birds and mice, or stalk other cats. This kitten is standing very still, ready to pounce.

The kittens are a month old and ready to drink from a bowl for the first time. They sniff the milk and stick their noses into it before they lap it up eagerly. They like their first taste of cat food too.

Tabitha spends a lot of time with her kittens, playing with them and watching them try new things. One of her kittens scrambles up a tree and then finds out that it's not so easy to get back down. It slips and hangs onto a branch before falling to the grass unhurt.

This kitten is learning to scratch a hole in the ground and then cover it over when it has finished going to the bathroom. Inside the house, it will do the same thing in a litter box.

The kittens never seem to get tired of playing with each other, or with any new toy they can find. All of this is wonderful exercise and they are growing stronger and bolder every day.

All of the kittens' playing is also practice for taking care of themselves when they grow up. This kitten is making a threatening gesture at us, arching its back and ruffling its fur. It has found a mouse that Tabitha caught and brought to her kittens. Cats are hunters by nature and Tabitha wants her kittens to learn how to hunt for themselves.

Even though the kittens are eating and drinking on their own, they still like to nurse. They are getting so large that there is no room for them to lie next to one another. Tabitha stands patiently while they nurse, but she is less and less willing as each day passes.

This warm summer night the kittens stay in the garden with Tabitha. In the morning we are surprised to see a prickly visitor from the woods join them for a bite to eat.

After they eat, the kittens care-
fully clean and groom themselves.
They don't need their mother to
take care of them anymore, and in
a few days they are each going to a
new home where they will grow up
loved as much as we love Tabitha.

EDUCATION

DATE DUE

MAY 1 6 1990	AUG 2 0 2008	
AUG		
MAY 2 2 1990		
RECEIVED MAY 1 8 1990		
JAN 1 5 1991		
RECEIVED DEC 2 0 1990		
SEP 1 6 1991		
RECEIVED SEP 1 6 1991		
JUL 2 7 1992		
RECEIVED JUL 2 2 1992		
NOV 0 9 1992	RECEIVED	
	AUG 0 9 2002	
MAR 1 9 1993		
SEP 2 3 1994		
RECEIVED SEP 2 2 1994		
OCT 1 8 1994		
RECEIVED OCT 1 8 1994		